THE SILENT WITNESS

HARSH RAJ

Made with ♥ on the Notion Press Platform
www.notionpress.com

Contents

Acknowledgements *v*

The Story *vii*

Important Characters *ix*

Backstory *xi*

1. The Witness 1

2. The Threats Begin 7

3. Detective Johnson 12

4. The Investigation 15

5. The Race Against Time 19

6. The Chase 22

7. The Truth 24

8. The Confrontation 26

9. The Aftermath 28

10. The Legacy 30

About The Author 33

Acknowledgements

This is my first ever full-fledged book published. So, I don't particularly have a team. This book is completely written, edited, formatted and outlined by me itself.

Though there were a lot online resources who helped me through the journey of the book publishing, as I didn't know anything about the process of publishing a book from scratch.

I would like to thanks my family and relatives too to encourage me through this phase.

And finally special thanks to Bethany Atazadeh who helped me through the complete guide to make this book possible.

THE STORY

"The Silent Witness" is a gripping thriller by Harsh Raj about a young woman named Amanda, who finds herself caught in a dangerous game of cat and mouse. Amanda is the only witness to a brutal murder that took place in the heart of the city New Orleans (The French Quarter), but she is too afraid to come forward and testify. The killer, a ruthless and cunning criminal, is determined to silence Amanda forever and stop her from speaking the truth.

With the help of a tenacious detective, Amanda must stay one step ahead of the killer while she struggles to come to terms with the horrors she has witnessed. As the body count rises and the stakes get higher, Amanda soon realizes that the only way to survive is to outwit the killer and bring him to justice.

Filled with twists and turns, "The Silent Witness" will keep you on the edge of your seat as Amanda races against time to uncover the truth and save herself from becoming the next victim.

Important Characters

In "The Silent Witness," there are a few important characters that drive the story forward:

1. Amanda - The young woman who is the only witness to a brutal murder and finds herself in the crosshairs of the killer.

2. Detective Johnson - A seasoned detective who is assigned to protect Amanda and bring the killer to justice. He is determined and dedicated to solving the case.

3. The Killer - A ruthless and cunning criminal who is determined to silence Amanda and stop her from speaking the truth.

4. Amanda's friends and family - They play a supporting role in the story and provide Amanda with a support system as she tries to navigate the dangerous situation, she finds herself in.

5. Witnesses and Suspects - Throughout the course of the story, other witnesses and suspects come forward, each with their own motives and secrets, adding to the suspense and making it harder for Amanda and Detective Johnson to solve the case.

BACKSTORY

I. Amanda

Amanda, the protagonist of "The Silent Witness," is a young woman in her mid-twenties who has had a difficult upbringing. Currently She Lives in New Orleans, US In a Very Clumsy Looking House. To Better Portray She Lives in The Heart of New Orleans "The French Quarter". Growing up, Amanda never had a stable home and was bounced from foster home to foster home. This instability left her with a deep-seated fear of abandonment and a distrust of authority figures. Despite these challenges, Amanda is a resilient and resourceful young woman who has learned to fend for herself.

Amanda has always been interested in art and has a passion for painting. She uses her art as a form of self-expression and a way to escape from the hardships of her everyday life. She Even Has her very own collection of very rare Art Type of "Photorealistic Paintings" whose worth can be way more than anyone can think of. But She couldn't Sell them Consists of Two Reasons. Firstly, She Cares Her Talent More Than Anything and Doesn't Want That Just for Some Amount of Money She Will Be Able to Shift the Ownership from Her to The Buyer. Secondly, Nobody Cared for Her Even to Look At her Paintings for Once Because Of Her Clumsy and Poor Condition.

However, Amanda's life takes a dark turn when she becomes the One And only witness to a brutal murder that takes place near her apartment building.

After the murder, Amanda is too scared to come forward and testify. She is afraid of retaliation from the killer and is also hesitant to trust the authorities As She

Never Ever Trusted Anyone from The Very Beginning Because She Was Always abandoned From Her Childhood. However, as the killer starts to close in on her, Amanda realizes that she has no choice but to come forward and speak the truth.

As the story progresses, Amanda begins to develop a bond with Detective Johnson, who is assigned to protect her. At first, she is hesitant to trust anyone, but as they start working together and a sense of cooperation starts building between them, she slowly starts to open up to Johnson and sees him as a father figure. Amanda's experiences also make her realize the importance of speaking out and standing up for what is right, even when it's scary. By Time She Understands That Social Anxiety or Trust Issues Is Somewhat Okay in A certain Limit, But When the Limits Are Crossed and You Have No Option Left You Must Choose the Appropriate Way to Fight Things Back.

Throughout the story, Amanda becomes a symbol of bravery and inspiration for others. Despite her traumatic experiences, she remains strong and determined to see the killer brought to justice, though she was very afraid in the beginning As She Was Not Able to Fight the Fear Withing Her. She Just Needed a Little Spark by Something or Someone to Take Over Fear Inside Her. That Spark Was Detective Johnson. By the end of the story, Amanda has grown and matured as a person, and she has a newfound sense of purpose and confidence. Now She Can live a purposeful life unlike before living in fear of trust and being abandoned.

II. Detective Johnson

Detective Johnson is a seasoned detective in his late forties who has been with the police force for over two decades. He comes from a working-class family and grew up in a rough neighborhood. Despite the challenges he faced in his upbringing, Detective Johnson was always driven and dedicated to serving his community.

As a young man, Detective Johnson was fascinated by detective work and dreamed of becoming a police officer. He worked hard to achieve his goal and quickly rose through the ranks, earning a reputation as one of the most dedicated and skilled detectives in the department.

Detective Johnson has seen it all in his long career, but he remains passionate about his work and dedicated to serving justice. He is a no-nonsense detective who is known for his tenacity and determination. However, despite his tough exterior. When Detective Johnson is assigned to protect Amanda, he sees her as just another case. However, as he starts to get to know her and learns about the traumatic experiences she has faced, he begins to feel a sense of responsibility towards her. He becomes determined to keep her safe and to bring the killer to justice.

Throughout the story, Detective Johnson and Amanda form a strong bond, and Detective Johnson comes to see Amanda as a daughter. He is proud of her bravery and is inspired by her determination. By the end of the story, Detective Johnson is hailed as a hero, but he remains humble and dedicated to his work. He continues to solve other cases, but he never forgets Amanda and the impact she had on his life.

I

THE WITNESS

Amanda was sitting in her small and clumsy apartment, surrounded by the familiar clutter of her life. She was working on a new painting, trying to capture the vivid colors of the sunset. As she mixed her paints, she felt a sense of calm wash over her. Painting was the one thing that always made her feel better, no matter what was going on in her life. It was the only way she could feel the sense of her living despite of too much hardships in her life. While painting she forgets about the darkness, weakness and all the irregularities of her life.

Suddenly, Amanda heard a loud bang coming from outside her window. The sound sensed as if there was a huge single arm attack just outside the window near to her where she was doing her painting work. She jumped up to clarify and see what was going on there, her heart started racing more than a speed of horse. Peering out the window, she saw a man, to be precise a dead man lying on the ground in the alley just below her apartment. She was completely shocked about what happened just now. Right Few Seconds Ago she was very calm and happy painting a beautiful scenery in her apartment, but the next moment she saw a horrifying incident that she was unable to process.

She Didn't know what to do now. Whether to go and check the person if he's alive or not, or whether to call an ambulance for him, or whether to shout like crazy to call up all neighbors around her. She found herself in a very critical condition. But then without thinking a second, she grabbed her phone and dialed 911.

"There's been a shooting!" she exclaimed, with her voice shaking. In a true horror and breaking voice, she cried over her phone "Please send help!"

"Kindly Elaborate Where's The Location Miss" in a hurry voice the police on call asked.

"The French Quarter in the down by alley, please hurry there's a lot of blood" Amanda Elaborated in a breaking and feared voice.

Within few minutes, police sirens filled the air, two police cars reached on the spot and Amanda watched them as a team of officers converged on the scene. They put "crime scene" tapes near the body. Soon body was carried away from there. One of the officers, a tall man with a stern face and brownish black hair, wearing an overcoat with goggles on his face, hands in his pockets approached her door.

"Ma'am, can you tell us what happened?" he asked, as Amanda let him into her apartment.

"I was sitting in my apartment near my window painting a scenery. Few seconds after I heard a loud Bang noise and looked out the window," Amanda explained, still in shock. "And th...th...then, Then I saw a m..m..m.. man lying on the ground." She Explained Stammering In her Voice.

The officer took out a notepad and started writing down her statement. As it is a very crucial part of any investigation to note down all the incidents that occurs, occurred or will be occurring in the following case. "Did you see who did it?" he asked.

Amanda shook her head. "No, I'm sorry, I couldn't see anything. It all happened so fast to be noticed by anyone."

"Well, we'll need you to come down to the station and make an official statement, without it we will not be able to continue with the further investigation" the officer said.

Amanda was not ready at all to agree on this as she didn't want to get involved in all of this. Her life was already like a hell, she didn't want to make it worse. But eventually remembering about what happened to the man, who's dead now, she agreed, and soon she found herself sitting in an interrogation room, facing a seasoned detective named Johnson.

"Miss, I'm Detective Johnson," he said, with a seriousness in his voice. "Can you tell me everything you saw and heard? The tiniest detail also that you remember can help this case take further."

Amanda took a deep breath and began to recount the events of the evening. "As I Already said, I was just painting when I heard a loud bang," she said. "And then I peered Out to see what that bang was there I saw a man lying on the ground, with lots of blood spilled on the floor."

Detective Johnson nodded, taking notes in his notebook. "Did you see anyone else around? In his apartment or anywhere near running away or staring or standing?"

Amanda shook her head. "No, I'm sorry. I didn't see anyone. At the time unfortunately I Was the only one who saw that terrifying crime or murder, I don't know how to describe it."

Detective Johnson sighed, clearly frustrated as he got no clues regarding the body, killer or the surrounding where the incident took place. "Well, we'll need to keep you in protective custody until we can find the person responsible for this dreadful murder," he said. "It's not safe for you to go back to your apartment, as if the killer knows that you have seen all the things that happened over there with your own eyes, he/she will think you as threat to disclose any sensitive information for him to be caught. Hence he would try to come after and eliminate you in order to survive and not be caught."

Amanda felt a wave of fear wash over her. She had never been in protective custody before, and the thought of being separated from her home and her things was frightening. As we already know about the nature of Amanda that she was afraid of getting abandoned as she spent almost all of her childhood from one house to another. Also, she didn't want to stay away from her home as she didn't completely know anything about the killer or the incident and wasn't completely sure that the killer will be identified by the police department or not.

But she also knew that she had no choice rather to stay in a protective custody, as she knew she was not capable of dealing with the killer alone if he showed up suddenly to her in her apartment. Also, she had seen something that could help the police catch a killer, as she really wanted these to get over as soon as possible and she had to do her part to help.

"Okay," she said, trying to sound brave, though she knew she isn't brave at all. "I'll do whatever it takes."

Detective Johnson gave her a reassuring smile. "You're doing the right thing, miss," he said. "We'll take care of you at any cost, just we need you to cooperate us and speak to us if you got to know anything or remembered anything about that incident."

And with that, Amanda's life was forever changed. From a simple life living girl minding her own business She had become a witness, a silent witness, to a brutal murder. And now she was determined to see the killer brought to justice, no matter what it took.

II

THE THREATS BEGIN

Amanda was given a small apartment in a secure building with bulletproof glasses around, round-the-clock police protection. Whatever she needed, she was provided with the stuff by a guard. But she was not allowed to go anywhere out without a police protection. Detective Johnson was assigned to be her primary protector, and he made it clear that he was taking his job seriously. He couldn't anything harm Amanda as she was the one and only witness to the murder. If anything happens to her this case will be closed forever and the killer will succeed in escaping the laws and this will be a big slap on the face of the whole police department. In any case detective Johnson didn't want any of these things happen. He never let his guard down in order to protect Amanda. Overall, Amanda was in a better place from before with a full high security. Where nothing could happen to her. Though there is a belief that wherever you go in this world or above the world whether be it heaven, nothing can take place of our very own home. Same thing could be felt by Amanda at those time.

For the first few days, Amanda was in a state of complete shock. She struggled to sleep properly. She had horrified dreams of that dead man and the killer trying to kill her. She wasn't able to take her meals properly, she couldn't even focus on painting, whenever she tries to imagine a beautiful scene or people to paint of, she always ends reminding of that incident that she witnessed with her own eyes. All she could think about was the shooting she had witnessed, the man she had seen lying on the ground. She even started thinking that if these things continue, she would end up like a schizophrenic patient seeing the killer and the dead man roaming near her and trying to kill her.

But then, the threats began. There were Mysterious phone calls in the middle of the night just for Amanda. Suspicious packages left outside her door. Each one sent a chill down Amanda's spine, reminding her that she was not safe. Finally, she understood that she is in the target of the killer and soon she will be eliminated if she or anyone in the department let their guard down for a moment.

Detective Johnson was relentless in his pursuit of the person responsible for the threats. He followed every lead, every clue, and interrogated every suspect. But no matter what he did, the threats continued.

One day, Detective Johnson received a tip from an informant. "I heard that there's a hit out on the witness," the informant said. "Someone's been hired to take her out."

Detective Johnson's blood ran cold. He had to keep Amanda safe, no matter what. He increased the security around her apartment, making sure that there was someone with her at all times.

Amanda was grateful for Detective Johnson's protection, but she was also starting to feel suffocated. She was tired of being cooped up in her small apartment, tired of feeling like a prisoner.

One night, after yet another threat, Amanda snapped. "I can't take it anymore!" she exclaimed. "I can't keep living like this!"

Detective Johnson tried to calm her down. "I know it's hard," he said. "But you have to stay strong. You're the only one who can help us catch the killer."

Amanda nodded, tears streaming down her face. She knew Detective Johnson was right, but she was also starting to feel like giving up.

But then, something happened that changed everything. Detective Johnson received a phone call from the informant, who had some new information.

"I heard that the person responsible for the threats is someone close to the witness," the informant said. "Someone she knows."

Detective Johnson's heart sank. He had suspected all along that the threats were coming from someone close to Amanda, but he had never been able to prove it.

Now, he was more determined than ever to catch the person responsible. He would do whatever it took to keep Amanda safe, and to bring the killer to justice.

And with that, the race against time was on. Detective Johnson and Amanda were both determined to find the truth, no matter what the cost.

III

DETECTIVE JOHNSON

Detective Johnson knew that he had to act fast. He spent the next few days investigating the new lead, interviewing Amanda's friends and family, and trying to gather as much evidence as possible.

At first, Amanda was hesitant to talk about her loved ones. She didn't want to believe that someone she knew could be responsible for the threats against her.

But Detective Johnson was persistent. He convinced her that they needed to look at everyone, no matter how painful it might be.

As they went through the list of Amanda's close friends and family, Detective Johnson noticed that one person kept coming up in the investigation: Amanda's ex-boyfriend, Michael.

Michael had always been jealous of Amanda's success as an artist. He had never been able to move on from their relationship, and had always been critical of her work.

Detective Johnson decided to pay Michael a visit. He brought along a team of officers and confronted Michael at his apartment.

Michael was taken by surprise. "What is this about?" he asked, his eyes wide with fear.

Detective Johnson didn't beat around the bush. "We have reason to believe that you're responsible for the threats against Amanda," he said.

Michael laughed nervously. "That's ridiculous," he said. "I wouldn't do something like that."

Detective Johnson wasn't convinced. He decided to take a closer look at Michael's phone records and online activity.

It didn't take long for Detective Johnson to find what he was looking for. Michael's phone records showed that he had made several calls to Amanda's apartment in the middle of the night. And his online activity showed that he had been searching for information on Amanda's location and police protection.

Detective Johnson arrested Michael on the spot. Amanda was shocked when she found out the news, but she was also relieved. She finally felt like she could breathe again.

Detective Johnson had solved the case. But he wasn't done yet. He wanted to make sure that Michael was prosecuted to the fullest extent of the law, so that Amanda would never have to worry about him again.

And with that, the case was finally closed. Detective Johnson was hailed as a hero, and Amanda was finally able to start putting the pieces of her life back together.

But Detective Johnson knew that he would never forget this case. It had changed him in ways he never could have imagined, and he would always carry the weight of Amanda's safety on his shoulders.

For Amanda, the future was finally starting to look bright. She was ready to get back to her life and her work, to start healing from the trauma of the past few months.

And for Detective Johnson, it was time to move on to the next case, to help another person in need. But he would always remember the silent witness, and the role he had played in keeping her safe.

IV

THE INVESTIGATION

Detective Johnson was relentless in his pursuit of the truth. He had made a promise to Amanda to keep her safe, and he intended to keep it. No matter what the circumstances are he was not ready to accept the defeat rather he was determined to bring the killer to justice.

The investigation into Michael's activities was intense. Detective Johnson and his team scoured through every detail of Michael's life, looking for any clues or evidence that could connect him to the threats against Amanda.

They were finally able to find a very crucial link between Michael and a man named Henry, who had a criminal record for harassment and extortion. Henry was the most wanted criminal who used to snatch all the money and worthy stuffs from the people on street. He even killed those people who denied to give money or from whom he didn't obtained anything.

Detective Johnson was stunned. He had never suspected that Michael would be working with someone else. He immediately brought Henry in for questioning as he was in the jail for his previous theft in the city.

Henry was defiant at first, refusing to answer any of Detective Johnson's questions. Henry was a strong will person anyhow he was not ready to open his mouth a bit that could lead anyone related to this case to any crucial clue to solve this case.

But Detective Johnson was patient. He was in no hurry, he just needed more logical aptitude to play with his mind. He knew that he had to break Henry down from tip to toe, to get to the truth. In spite of everything the detective tried on henry, he didn't spoke a single bit from his mouth.

Then Detective Johnson Had to Use Most Powerful Weapon for Criminals "Falsifying A Bail".

Slowly but surely, Henry started to crack. He revealed that Michael had approached him, offering him money to intimidate Amanda. Henry had accepted the offer, thinking that it was an easy way to make some quick cash, as these criminals can do anything for a handsome amount of money.

But as the threats escalated, Henry started to feel nervous. He didn't want to get caught once again, and he didn't want to be responsible for anything that might happen to Amanda.

That's when Henry turned to Detective Johnson for help. He was willing to testify against Michael in exchange for a lighter sentence.

Detective Johnson agreed to the deal, and the investigation was finally starting to come together. They had the evidence they needed to build a strong case against Michael.

Amanda was overjoyed when she heard the news. She couldn't believe that the nightmare was finally coming to an end.

Detective Johnson and his team worked tirelessly, putting together a case that was solid and irrefutable. They were finally ready to take Michael to court.

The trial was a long and difficult process, but in the end, justice was served. Michael was found guilty of all charges, and he was sentenced to a long prison term.

Amanda was finally free from the threat of harm. She was able to move on with her life, knowing that she was safe and protected.

And Detective Johnson was finally able to close the case, knowing that he had kept his promise to Amanda. He was proud of the work he had done, and he was grateful for the opportunity to help someone in need.

For Amanda and Detective Johnson, the future was finally looking bright. They had both been through a long and difficult journey, but they had come out stronger on the other side. And they both knew that they would never forget the journey they had been on, or the role they had played in each other's lives.

V

THE RACE AGAINST TIME

Detective Johnson was feeling the pressure. He had received a call from Amanda, telling him that she had received another threat. This time, the threat was more serious and more immediate.

Amanda was scared, and Detective Johnson could hear the fear in her voice. He knew that he had to act fast, before it was too late.

He immediately called in his team, and they started working on the case. They had to find the source of the threat, and they had to do it quickly.

As they worked, Detective Johnson realized that they were in a race against time. The threat was real, and it was imminent.

He put all of his focus and energy into the case, determined to find the person responsible. He worked through the night, pouring over every piece of evidence and every detail.

Finally, after hours of intense work, Detective Johnson had a breakthrough. He found a clue that led him to a man named James, who had a history of making threats and carrying out acts of violence.

Detective Johnson and his team moved quickly, bringing James in for questioning. But James was defiant, refusing to answer any of Detective Johnson's questions.

Detective Johnson knew that he had to be creative. He had to find a way to get James to talk, to reveal the truth.

He started playing mind games with James, slowly wearing him down and making him feel vulnerable. And finally, James broke. He revealed that he had been hired by Michael's former business partner, who was seeking revenge against Michael and anyone associated with him.

Detective Johnson was shocked. He had never suspected that the threat would come from someone so close to Michael. He immediately put a plan into action, working with Amanda to keep her safe and secure.

As they worked, Detective Johnson could feel the clock ticking down. He knew that he had to be quick, before it was too late.

But in the end, his hard work paid off. He was able to track down the business partner, and he was able to bring him to justice.

Amanda was finally free from the threat of harm, and she was able to start over with her life. And Detective Johnson was finally able to close the case, knowing that he had done everything in his power to protect the people he cared about.

For Detective Johnson, it was a reminder of the importance of his work, and of the people he was working to protect. He was proud of what he had accomplished, and he was grateful for the opportunity to make a difference in someone's life.

VI

THE CHASE

Detective Johnson was on the move. He had received word that James had escaped from custody, and he was determined to bring him back in. As Always, he never missed a chance to let any criminal get off and free from the custody.

He gathered his team, and they headed out into the city, searching for any sign of James. They followed leads and tips, and they finally found a trail that led them to the outskirts of town.

As they approached a run-down warehouse, Detective Johnson knew that they had found James. He motioned for his team to take up positions, and he quietly made his way inside.

He could hear James moving around inside, and he knew that he had to act fast. He crept through the darkness, his gun at the ready, and he finally caught a glimpse of James up ahead.

Without hesitation, Detective Johnson sprang into action. He raced towards James, shouting for him to surrender.

But James was not going to go down without a fight. He pulled out a gun, and he fired at Detective Johnson.

Detective Johnson ducked behind a stack of crates, returning fire. The two men exchanged shots, and Detective Johnson could feel the tension building. He knew that this was a life-or-death situation, and he had to be careful.

Finally, after what felt like an eternity, Detective Johnson got the upper hand. He was able to disarm James, and he took him into custody.

As they made their way back to the police station, Detective Johnson could feel the weight lifting from his shoulders. He had done what he had set out to do, and he had brought James to justice.

But he also knew that his work was far from over. There were always more cases to solve, and more people to protect. And for Detective Johnson, that was just fine. He was a detective, through and through, and he was always ready for the next challenge.

VII

THE TRUTH

Amanda sat nervously in the interrogation room; her hands clasped together tightly in her lap. Detective Johnson sat across from her; his eyes fixed on her as he began to speak.

"Amanda, we need to talk about what really happened that night," Detective Johnson said.

Amanda took a deep breath and nodded. She had been dreading this moment for weeks, but she knew that she couldn't keep the truth from Detective Johnson any longer.

"I know that I lied to you before, about what I saw on the night of the murder," Amanda said, her voice shaking. "I saw James at the scene of the crime. He was covered in blood, and he was holding a knife."

Detective Johnson leaned forward; his eyes intense. "Why didn't you tell me this before?" he asked.

"I was scared," Amanda said, tears starting to fill her eyes. "James threatened me. He told me that if I said anything, he would hurt my family. I didn't know what to do. I was so scared."

Detective Johnson reached across the table and took Amanda's hand. "It's going to be okay, Amanda," he said.

"We're going to make sure that James pays for what he's done, and that you and your family are protected."

Amanda nodded, her eyes filling with gratitude. She knew that Detective Johnson was a man of his word, and she felt a sense of comfort knowing that he was on her side.

As Detective Johnson rose from his seat, he looked down at Amanda with a stern expression. "We're going to get to the bottom of this, Amanda," he said. "And we're going to bring James to justice. No matter what it takes."

Amanda watched as Detective Johnson walked out of the room, and she felt a sense of hope for the first time in weeks. She knew that Detective Johnson would do everything in his power to protect her and bring James to justice, and that gave her the strength to keep going.

VIII

THE CONFRONTATION

Detective Johnson sat across from James in the interrogation room, his eyes fixed on the man who had caused so much pain and fear.

"James, we have evidence that puts you at the scene of the crime," Detective Johnson said, his voice stern. "And we have Amanda's testimony that puts you there with a knife in your hand."

James sneered at Detective Johnson. "I don't know what you're talking about," he said.

Detective Johnson leaned forward, his eyes blazing. "Don't play games with me, James. You know exactly what I'm talking about. You murdered a man in cold blood, and now it's time for you to pay for what you've done."

James leaned back in his chair, a smirk on his face. "You have nothing on me, Detective," he said. "And even if you did, I have friends in high places. You'll never be able to make this stick."

Detective Johnson didn't back down. He stood up from his seat, his voice rising. "We have all the evidence we need, James. And I'm not afraid to use it. I'm going to make sure that you pay for what you've done, even if it takes me the rest of my life."

James's expression changed, his smile turning into a snarl. "You'll never take me down, Detective. I've always been one step ahead of you. And I'll always be one step ahead of you."

Detective Johnson reached across the table, his hand closing into a fist. "We'll see about that, James. We'll see who comes out on top in the end."

And with that, Detective Johnson walked out of the interrogation room, his mind racing as he tried to figure out his next move. He knew that James was a dangerous man, and he wouldn't stop until he was brought to justice. But Detective Johnson was determined to make that happen, no matter what the cost.

IX

THE AFTERMATH

Detective Johnson sat in his office, his mind still racing with the events of the past few days. He had finally caught James, the man who had murdered a young man in cold blood. But even with James behind bars, Detective Johnson couldn't shake the feeling that there was more to the story.

He was pulled out of his thoughts by a knock at the door. He looked up to see Amanda standing in the doorway, a small smile on her face.

"Detective Johnson, I wanted to thank you," Amanda said, her voice trembling with emotion. "You caught the man who murdered my brother, and I can finally have some peace knowing that justice has been served."

Detective Johnson stood up from his desk and walked over to Amanda, giving her a hug. "I'm just glad I could help," he said, his voice warm. "But it wasn't just me. It was a team effort, and we couldn't have done it without you."

Amanda pulled away from the hug, her smile growing. "I'm just happy that it's over," she said. "I can finally move on from this tragedy and start to heal."

Detective Johnson nodded, his mind already moving on to the next case. "That's what's important," he said. "Moving forward and finding peace. I'm here if you need anything, Amanda. And I'm sure that your brother is looking down on you, proud of the strength you've shown."

Amanda nodded, tears welling up in her eyes. "Thank you, Detective," she said. "I'll never forget what you've done for me and my family."

And with that, Amanda turned and walked out of Detective Johnson's office, leaving him alone with his thoughts once again. But this time, he was at peace knowing that he had helped bring closure to a family in need, and that was all that mattered to him.

X

THE LEGACY

One year had passed since the events of The Silent Witness case, and Detective Johnson was called to a small park on the outskirts of town. When he arrived, he saw Amanda sitting on a bench, a small smile on her face.

"Detective Johnson," Amanda said, standing up as he approached. "I wanted to show you something."

Detective Johnson followed Amanda to the center of the park, where a plaque had been erected. It read, "In memory of John Doe, taken too soon. His legacy lives on through the bravery and determination of those who fought for justice."

Detective Johnson felt a lump form in his throat as he read the plaque. He remembered the young man who had been taken from this world too soon, and he was grateful to have played a part in bringing his murderer to justice.

"I wanted to thank you again," Amanda said, her voice choked with emotion. "You were instrumental in bringing justice for my brother, and I'll always be grateful for that."

Detective Johnson placed a hand on Amanda's shoulder. "It was my pleasure," he said, his voice sincere. "I'm just glad I could help."

Amanda smiled, her eyes shining with gratitude. "This park is going to be a safe haven for families in the community," she said. "A place where they can come and remember their loved ones and find peace."

Detective Johnson nodded, his heart swelling with pride. He knew that he had made a difference in Amanda's life and in the lives of many others.

"You know, Amanda," Detective Johnson said, his voice soft. "I've been a detective for a long time, but this case will always stand out to me. Not just because we caught the murderer, but because of the strength and determination you showed. Your brother would be proud of you."

Amanda's eyes filled with tears as she looked up at Detective Johnson. "Thank you," she said, her voice shaking with emotion. "That means more to me than you can ever know."

And with that, Amanda turned and walked away, leaving Detective Johnson to stand in the park and reflect on the legacy of The Silent Witness. He knew that this case would stay with him for the rest of his life, a reminder of the bravery of one young woman and the power of justice.

About The Author

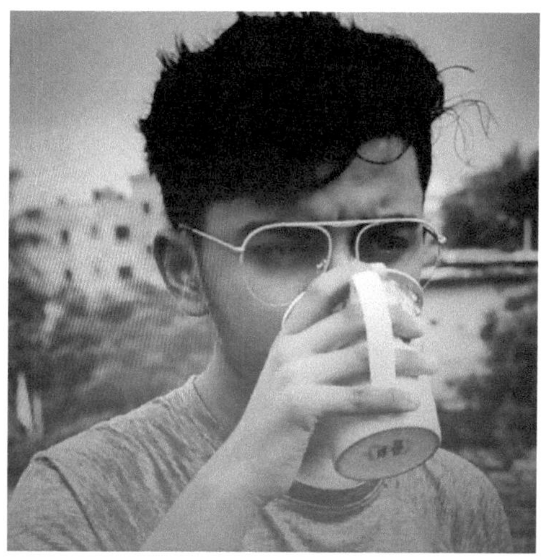

Photo © 2020 Harsh Raj

I am a student currently studying multimedia and game design. Also, I make short films and movies. In this creative process a lot of ideas are required. Hence I get a lot of ideas to create something. Therefore, I am starting my journey of keeping all my ideas intact in the form books. In this journey the ideas will be delivered to you readers also to get chills and enjoyment.

Printed by Libri Plureos GmbH in Hamburg,
Germany